Riding *the* Rails

Mc Graw Hill SRA

Columbus, OH

SRAonline.com

Send all inquiries to this address:
SRA/McGraw-Hill
4400 Easton Commons
Columbus, OH 43219

ISBN: 978-0-07-608779-2
MHID: 0-07-608779-4

1 2 3 4 5 6 7 8 9 NOR 13 12 11 10 09 08 07

The McGraw-Hill Companies

The Gold Rush of 1849 was over. People still went to California to find prosperity, though. Sarah and Emily's father wanted to do the same.

Mr. Miller worked for a trading company. He bought and sold goods. He planned to run his own business in the West. In 1881 he decided to move there.

Sarah and Emily lived in Chicago. They were used to busy city life. They were not happy about moving to California.

"Father!" Emily cried.

"Our friends live here!" Sarah said.

Thousands of people were heading to California. Mr. Miller planned to start his business in San Francisco. He knew the city would soon be booming with overseas trade. Mr. Miller also understood Sarah and Emily's fears.

"I know how you feel," he said. "Your mother and I left England to come here. We were afraid to leave our families. But once we arrived as immigrants in America, there were so many new things to see. I still miss my family. But I grew to love our new country."

Friends came to see the Millers off. After tearful good-byes, the family boarded the train for the six-day trip.

Some of the trains were not very comfortable, but the Pullman train cars were large. The sleeping cars had beds that folded down. Meals were served in the dining car. Passengers could relax on padded chairs or sofas.

The train engines were called iron horses because they had replaced live horses as the best way to travel.

"All aboard!" the conductor shouted, and the train pulled out of the station.

As the girls settled into their seats and looked out the large window, the iron horse rolled westward.

The prairie stretched for miles and miles. Sarah spotted movement in the sea of tall grass.

"Look, Father, a herd of buffalo!" she exclaimed.

"Before the railroad was built there were millions of buffalo," Mr. Miller said. "But the railroad workers had to kill them for food. There aren't as many left now."

The train stopped for water, and the small herd disappeared over a bluff.

The train chugged across Iowa and into Nebraska. Emily and Sarah saw more animals. They saw antelope, buffalo, deer, and even small prairie dogs.

"I've never seen so many wild animals," Sarah whispered.

Then the train crossed the Platte River. It had been a water route for the Pony Express. People who had traveled west in wagons had crossed it. Now the river was a place to get water for the iron horse. It ran on steam so it needed water regularly.

Most towns along the railroad tracks were filled with people, but some towns were empty. In those towns miners or railroad workers once walked the streets. They left when there was no more work.

The train stopped in Wyoming. As Sarah and Emily walked around, they saw many American Indians.

"The Sioux and Cheyenne live here," Mrs. Miller said. "Once they were the only people who lived out here. Now that the railroad brings people from the East, many of them have lost their land."

The train was on its way again, and the prairie gave way to mountains.

"These are the Rocky Mountains," Mr. Miller said. "It must have been very hard for settlers to cross this mountain region on foot."

"There's snow on the mountains!" Emily yelled.

"That's the highest point on the railway," the conductor shouted.

The girls were thrilled when they saw towering mountains, deep canyons, and wooden bridges that looked as though they could not hold the weight of the heavy iron horse.

Sarah was afraid of crossing the bridges. "They look so rickety," she said.

"Wait until we go through a tunnel," the conductor said, smiling.

The first tunnel was in Utah.

"It's so dark," Emily said, "and the train's echo is *so* loud. Isn't this exciting?"

Sarah was happy when the sunlight reappeared, though. The iron horse headed toward Echo Canyon. The steep ravines, huge boulders, and high cliffs were beautiful.

"I can't imagine traveling this region in wagon trains," Mrs. Miller said.

Emily loved Utah. "The rocks are shaped like towers and castles!" she said. During the evening the train traveled through Utah. Then it entered Weber Canyon. The canyon was surrounded with more huge rocks.

The train then went through Promontory Point. There the Central Pacific and Union Pacific railroads met. It was the spot where the last spike was hammered into the rails to complete the railroad.

Sunset over the Great Salt Lake was lovely. It sparkled purple against a red sky. The air smelled of salt and other minerals.

In Nevada the train crossed the desert. Cactus and sagebrush spotted the treeless mountains. Lizards scampered to find shade. During stops, hot, dry air blasted into the train cars.

At Humboldt Station the passengers got off to stretch. There Mr. Miller treated the girls to tall glasses of icy-cold tea. It was mixed with just a little sugar. Emily and Sarah quickly drank it down.

Later black clouds and rumbling thunder filled the sky. The rain released the smell of desert sage.

"It's such a different world," Sarah whispered as she drifted off to sleep.

Climbing the rocky Sierras was not easy for the iron horse. The tracks hugged the mountain wall. Emily looked out of the window and saw that the ground dropped down into a bottomless pit.

The train made its way through several snow sheds, which had been built to keep snow off the tracks.

The rocking of the train as it wound its way through the mountains woke Sarah. The train was rounding Cape Horn, one of the greatest cliffs in the Sierras.

"We're up so high!" Sarah said, grinning.

Then the view opened wide, and the girls saw a green valley filled with flowers, cornfields, and fruit trees.

Emily and Sarah gazed out, thinking about their new life. They were far from home and were going to start a new life. The thought was a bit scary, but the possibilities were endless.

Their long trek ended at the San Francisco Bay. Mr. Miller announced, "We have reached our destination!"

"I cannot believe all the amazing things we have seen on this trip," Sarah said. Emily agreed. For them this first train trip was a new beginning.

The Millers were ready to start their new lives. Living in a new town and meeting new people was going to be a challenge, but they had just crossed half the continent. After that they felt ready for *any* challenge!

Vocabulary

prosperity (pros per´ i tē) (page 3) *n.* Success, wealth, or good fortune.

immigrants (i´ mi grənts) (page 4) *n.* Plural of **immigrant:** A person who comes to live in a country in which he or she was not born.

prairie (prâ´ rē) (page 6) *n.* A large area of level or rolling land with grass and few or no trees.

region (rē´ jən) (page 9) *n.* Any large area or territory.

rickety (ri´ ki tē) (page 10) *adj.* Likely to fall or break; shaky.

minerals (min´ ər əls) (page 11) *n.* Plural of **mineral:** A substance found in nature that is not an animal or plant. Salt, coal, and gold are minerals.

challenge (chal´ ənj) (page 15) *n.* A call to take part in a difficult task or contest.

Comprehension Focus: Visualizing

1. Visualize yourself in the desert described on page 12. Write three sentences about what it might be like to be there.

2. Reread page 11. Draw a picture of how you visualize a scene on the page.